My Journey

Manish Kumar Sinha

ISBN 978-93-5458-596-8

Published in India 2021 by Pencil

A brand of
One Point Six Technologies Pvt. Ltd.
123, Building J2, Shram Seva Premises,
Wadala Truck Terminal, Wadala (E)
Mumbai 400037, Maharashtra, INDIA
E connect@thepencilapp.com
W www.thepencilapp.com

DISCLAIMER: *This is a work of fiction. Names, characters, places, events and incidents are the products of the author's imagination. The opinions expressed in this book do not seek to reflect the views of the Publisher.*

Author biography

A common man having a dream of achieving big. Done my B.Tech in CS from Kuvemput University and was my passing my days as any other software professional would do, earning big and slogging out from 9 to 9 until i decided to try something for myself; My passion.

CONTENTS

COURAGE

Every individual can interpret the meaning of Courage in different ways. I suppose all of them are correct in their own paradigm.

For some this is physical strength, for some the endurance level, for many of us talking and writing about something wrong which is happening with anyone or anywhere....

I am not sure how many of us rate ourselves as which category of individual we are in terms of defining courage, but I know I am the one who falls under the category where courage is all about discussing with my friend and group about what is ethically right.

Those were the golden days of my childhood and Teen when I was in school with white shirt and blue half pant as my uniform (By the way I carried on with half pant till standard 9th which was embarrassing even by the standard of mid 80's). We just finished our school and as expected from a middle class or lower middle-class student, I was supposed to be an engineer. To fulfil this dream, I must join some coaching class in Patna or Delhi based on the income of my parent.

I am not sure whose dream it was to become an engineer, mine? or my parents?

Let us argue that I have the dream of becoming an engineer then what about those dreams of being a Gladrag model (common guys not joking, weighing just 45 - 50 kg and so lean and thin that I could start floating in air if the wind blows in an effective way :), but then people used to tell that you look good), or being a fighter pilot or an actor like Amitabh Bacchan and run around trees romancing with gorgeous girls........never ending list.

What if I say my parent's dream, really was it?

I assume this idea emerged from the society itself as that was the most efficient and optimized way to earn a respectful and stable livelihood.

Anyway, I took admission at a coaching centre in Patna along with 3 of my best friends from school. After all what is life without the company of friends. Life at coaching center is itself a hilarious incident which I will write about in a separate topic.

I, Manish, Punit and Shekhar sharing two rooms and started our journey to be an engineer from IIT (Nothing less from IIT is what everyone targets for, right?).

Daily we use to cook different dishes eat a lot, do all those teen-age mischievous things and spent those hard-earned money of our parent happily and at the end study a bit. Every morning we eat our breakfast (Very fond of poori jalebi) at a nearby cheap dhaba go to our coaching class and try to understand how come Resnick and Halliday could have understood such difficult problem of physics :(and come back to our room roaming around the Patna market.

It was one of those regular days I, Manish and Punit were coming back to our room after our class. We were talking, laughing and staring at those beautiful girls passing by. Touching hands of those girls and pretending as if they were unintentional :).

We were passing by a shoe house; a little boy came

running from inside the shop to throw away some garbage. His hand painted in black because of collecting dump and garbage while cleaning the shop. He was in hurry and nearly avoided bumping us. We went few steps only when we heard some noise and the boy crying. We turned and saw that young boy bumped into another passer-by; a heavy bully well-built 6- footer. That man slapped him and started abusing, saying can't you walk properly.

I and Punit were feeling sorry for this and started discussing with our self as others around that boy and man, how come that guy slap him when he was not at fault? Boy was in hurry to clean the shop and throw away garbage and while rushing outside it was mere chance that he collided with him, to avoid collision he put his hand in front because of which that man's shirt was spoiled. We were discussing all those ethically right things and feeling sorry for that boy.

Suddenly we saw Manish rushing towards that Man who slapped this young boy and caught his hand. He questioned him why he slapped? and the guy said all those things like look at my shirt he has spoiled it. Manish told him, boy is not at fault he never did it deliberately and the man started shouting at manish. Who are you to talk for this boy are you his uncle or something? Go away or I will thrash you like anything, suddenly manish took the hand of that boy in his hand and rubbed it all on his shirt everywhere. He caught that man's collar and yelled at him now do whatever you want to do. Man was shocked at Manish's courage which his physical strength could not match, and he started shouting come at Patna college gate and I will see you...

Manish told come let's go wherever you want to and see

what you can do, after few minutes people started gathering and they settled it down and we three again started making fun out of ourselves, laughing talking and trying to touch few of those beautiful girls passing by....

BADREE

Every educated person...uhm...Not every let's say most of the educated person do know about the slavery system of earlier days in United States and how much pain people of America took to end this horrible system.

How many of you have read that epic novel Gone with the wind, it gives a glimpse into a different perspective of that horrible slavery system for me. I am not trying to defend anything here guys, do not start thinking in other way. I am just saying that even under the most horrible of system and circumstances humanity exists.

Indians cannot differentiate based on colour as all of them are either brown or dark brown :). Cast and economic condition do play a major role in defining your status of slavery (Yes all of us are slaves in one way or other).

For me that timespan was one of the defining moments in my life (whenever I look behind and analyse) where I surprised myself as how I acted when my idealism met with abstract reality. How every pillar of my self-righteousness fell to dirt in a very miserable way with the slightest touch of reality.

We three brothers and sisters were growing up together in a very cosy and comfortable environment provided for by our parents. I could always boast of the way I was nurtured into a human being who tends to care about others as well, and I still am very proud of this because I know there are very few people who are like that. These values which I carry with myself are partly because of me but mostly because of the way my parent and family educated me, my friends discussed with me and the teachers who taught me. Whenever I used to see people doing some injustice to helpless poor people, domestic helps...I used to curse and feel bad for them, I use to hate those people who do such things in life.

My family used to live in a small township created by Coal India for its employees called NTS Barkakana, my ancestral home was situated in a remote area (at that time) of Bihar called Jhanjharpur. Since we were growing and the work pressure on my mother was increasing my parent decided to bring a domestic help from Jhanjharpur. Because of poor economic condition of people in that remote village availability of people who could work as domestic help was immense. We decided to bring a boy named Badree with us to Barkakana (Guys that was way back in 80's when I am not sure if any child labour law exists and even if it exists people cared about it).

Badree was very young (around 14-15 years old) and energetic boy and was excited to come with us as he has never been out of his village and he was knowing that he will be provided with quality of life which he could never imagine living there in the village.

He was very happy and comfortable playing with me and talking to me and we grow a kind of bond between ourselves. He started living with us and my family use to take good care of Badree.

Being new for household work he spends most of his time with my mother learning all the details and once we come back from school he uses to spent as much of his time with me as he could find from his busy schedule.

He used to sleep beside me on a separate cot, and I noticed that during night lot of mosquitoes around his body, yet he used to sleep comfortably. I was sleeping inside mosquito net and my inner self started raising his voice against this injustice. I asked my mother why we do not get him a mosquito net and she told "beta they are habitual of sleeping like this comfortably", but I argued that they might be sleeping in worse condition there at their home, but we need to provide him with a mosquito net. My mother agreed and she brought an old net which was torn at different places for him and I was so happy that I did the right thing. We three even got some books for him so that he can learn reading and writing, and we use to teach him alphabets and read through the story books.

As time goes by our inner self used to raise less and less of those voices as we were getting accustomed to Badree working for us and may be the darker side overtaking those voices.

One day my father came from office very tired and asked Badree to massage him, my mother told Badree to go and massage him. We were studying in a different room; I took a break from my study and was going to kitchen for some water and I saw Badree sitting on my bed and doing massage. There was a kind of anger or uneasiness inside me when I saw him on my bed sitting. I was thinking how could he (a house help) can sit on my bed? he can massage my father standing on the floor what was the need for him to go on my bed and make it dirty...or should I say how could a servant step on his master's bed? I rushed to my mother in anger and asked her Ma why Badree is sitting on my bed? My mother told me common how he is supposed to massage your father without climbing on bed? And why you are so angry about it if he is sitting on his bed...I told her how a servant can sit on my bed. My mother got angry on this and scolded me off from there. I was not able to digest that fact...Now I recollect that time period and I visualize that I started discriminating with Badree in regular day to day activities more than my parents would do without realizing at that point that I am doing that. Badree would have felt those changes in me.

One fine day that discrimination reached to an ugly incident when I realized how your own idealism gets shattered in front of reality, how you start enjoying the power and position and start acting irresponsibly.

It was a weekend and my mother told Badree to wash our school dress for the next week. Badree did so in the afternoon and put it on hanger for drying. Mother asked us to get the school dress and press it. We collected our school dress from hanger for press, I noticed that my trouser was in very bad shape full of wrinkles whereas the dress of my sisters were normal and were in perfect crease after a light press. I pressed my trouser to remove the wrinkles, but they just persisted, I was so angry at Badree. I shouted and called him up asking what he did to my pant, my mother also came. I scolded him so much in front of everyone that he started crying. My mother asked me to stop shouting and very respectfully asked Badree what happened why there are so many wrinkles on my trouser, crying Badree told that while washing he felt that he should wash my trouser better and cleaner (as he is fond of me and plays with me) so he washed my trouser with hot water and after squeezing out water from the cloth he put it on hanger for drying. As the trouser was washed with hot water and squeezed the wrinkles were very hard on the cloth.

I was standing there stunned with the explanation.

CAKE

How greedy you can be?

Can ever being greedy would bring those happy memories which you think about and laugh your heart out? I am not sure about others, but I have one of those which I am sharing here.

Those were those good old coaching days when we were trying to be the best Engineers which India can produce, no pun intended here guys...

Most of the Bihari bachelor boys you meet or friend with you will find one common quality in them (I know they all are preparing for the IAS, I am also a Bihari, so I very well know about this), most of them are good cook.

We four friends use to live together in a rented room. I, Manish and Shekhar were taking coaching classes for IIT and Punit was doing it for AIIMS. Our classes start at the same time but Punit returns to the room at different time than us. How much effort we put on our studies is something I can argue upon later with a defensive mindset but our effort to prepare our daily meal was one thing where no one can put us on Backfoot. Punit was good at making dough, I was crafty in making chapatis and Manish's soybean Potato used to be delicious (on a side note he prepare the same combination way more than our liking).

One fine day I could not remember how or why but we

decided to prepare cake for ourselves. We came back from our classes and went to market to buy all the ingredients for cake. Next day morning we all started with very determined and focused approach to prepare cake. All those guys or girls who are from non- metro cities and from lower middle-class background knows the trick of making cake using Hawkins pressure cooker :)

We prepared the dough and put egg and baking powder and started battering and mixing the dough again and again and again and.....

People you must understand that our cooking abilities were on stake we cannot let that go, our cake must be the softest and spongiest cake anyone can make. Until our arms started telling us enough, we were mixing and battering.

Then we prepared the cooker by putting brown paper and buttering it so that the base of our cake does not stick and burn out. Then we put the mixture spread it out evenly and put the cooker on stove on very mild flame to bake properly.

We waited very impatiently for the duration to complete so that we can open the cooker and see how much it has sponged out or is it going to be a disastrous chapati like thing.

We opened the lid as if we are looking at our results of IIT/Aims and.....

WOW

What we were looking at was one of the spongiest golden-brown cake mankind has ever made.

Next moment we saw Punit with a lock and key of his trunk, he put the lid back on cooker and put the whole cooker inside his trunk and locked it and kept the key in his pocket and started laughing. I do not believe you dogs, your class end before mine and you are not going to leave anything for me when I am back. We will open this trunk when we all are at room and will enjoy it together.

That day the class was longest and never ending, anyhow it ended, and we reached our room. After some time Punit came in rushing.

We opened the trunk and removed the cake out from cooker very carefully. Looking at the mere shape of our cake we were so ecstatic.

We cut the cake and... Inside we could see the big honeycomb like structure. We all looked at each other and all of us were having a very sheepish smile on our faces, probably we knew what is going to happen. We all took our halves and put a bite in our mouth and..........

YES, it was a disaster, our mouth was filled with the taste of soda and we started laughing madly looking at the cake and each other.

In our over enthusiasm we have overdone the quantity of baking soda.

SONPUR KA MELA

Sonpur is place nearby Patna on the bank of river Ganges. Sonpur is famous for organizing biggest cattle fair of Asia and stretches from Fifteen days to a Month. Sonpur mela is held on Karthik Poornima (Full moon day) in the month of November – December.

It has its origins during the time of Chandragupta Maurya who used to buy elephants and horses across the river Ganges.

We heard a lot about this mela from our childhood and how popular it is, you can find almost any animal there. I never had a chance to see this mela but heard a lot about it from people and friends. During recent times this mela has become more popular for it's mischievous 'Nautanki' and I along with my friends heard a lot of erotic stories about those Nautankis which are held at different tents during Sonpur mela.

I along with my friends Punit, Manish and Shekhar were in Patna doing our coaching during that time of November – December when Sonpur mela was going on. This was once in a lifetime opportunity for us to go and see the mela and authenticate those stories which we have heard from our friends.

Everything was in place and we planned everything to the perfection so that our parents do not know that we are visiting this mela (because of the bad reputation those

'Nautankis' have pinned on to this mela). One thing is sure in life and that is surprises as it makes your life worth living and adventurous, so however you plan and whatever way the best plan you put forth there are bound to be surprises. Our PG front door closes at around 9:00 PM every day and the PG owner close the door after 9:00 PM and do not open it for anyone. We planned our journey in such a way that we should be back by 9:00 PM so that no one knows and inform our parents about we not being there in the PG.

We were having two travel options from Patna to Sonpur, first one was travelling via Bus and the second one was through boat along the river Ganges. We decided to take bus while going and use boat service while returning.

Early morning, we take our backpack and reached Sonpur mela at around 10:00 AM. It was so big and crowded we never imagined that a mela could be such big and full of life. We were roaming around merrily looking at different stalls and breeds of animals available for sale. We started searching for stalls where they have elephants for sale, I never saw a real elephant on sale. I mean we as Indian kid have seen elephants roaming around on road or small fest meant for elephant ride but never saw one standing in stall for sale and purchase (Well apart from chicken and some other small birds and dogs I do not think that I have ever seen any other animal for sale but elephant brings a different kind of curiosity as they are so big and kind of peculiar for me to be available in some kind of fest for sale and purchase), so we decided to look out for stalls where elephant are there. We reached almost to the end of the area where we could find few elephants standing for the transaction. It was almost around 3:00 PM when we decide enough of 'Aawaragardi' and started looking out for those tents where we can go and watch those 'Nautankis' and verify about the trueness of those stories we have heard earlier. Soon we found a banner with a very erotically dressed woman taking most of the area and on the side footnote there was something written. We were so excited and giggling looking at each other and the poster, suddenly Punit pointed out about the footnote.

Guys read the timings, and we all were sad and dejected.

Nautanki shows were supposed to start past 9:00 PM, but we never lost out hope and decided to look out for other option thinking there must be somewhere with a timing which suits our plan. With each new banner images of different girls with those erotic dress changed, but the timing remains consistent.

Adventure also has its limit defined with the person or group who is indulged, for our group at that time and age going to Sonpur and watching Nautaki was the limit to our adventure (without our parent and PG owner knowing about it), but spending the entire night out of PG and our parent knowing about it was something our mind was not trained at that time to imagine. After a lot of discussion and argument we decided that we should be leaving Sonpur if we want to reach our PG before 9:00 PM so that the doors are not closed.

Now when I think about that incident, I am not sure but sounds way too kiddish that we were afraid of knocking at the PG door for the Owner to open (Owner was having very bad reputation of shouting at people who do not follow his rules). Even if he reported the incident to our parents, we could have made many excuses about our being late but.....

Boat journey was already a planned adventure while returning from Sonpur, so we rushed towards the Ghats of Ganges where the boats were ready to take people to the other side of Ganges (Across the River Ganges are the two cities of Sonpur and Patna).

We boarded the boat and started our boat journey on the Ganges, Cold and cozy breeze flowing across our faces were soothing out our nerves and removed those disappointment of not watching Nautanki. After some time, we guys again started chattering and laughing at each other talking about the events of the entire day, time going by and soon we realized that the decision to return via boat was not good as it was taking a lot of time. And then from the Ghat to the PG we must travel which will again take more time.

As we reached the other side we jumped and started running to catch an auto to beat the time to reach PG. But when something must go wrong it will go wrong and that happened to us, by the time we reached PG door it was way too late, and the gates were closed already.

We all were in panic thinking what should we do? Where we are going to spend our night?

PG was built in such a way that an 8 ft. wall was surrounding the building of the PG and there was an entry door. About 1 ft. over the boundary wall there was a mesh of live high voltage electricity wires.

With no other option we decided to dare and climb over the wall and go inside the PG without anyone knowing. We decided to climb on the back of other guy and cross the wall and again from the other side of the wall someone will climb on the back of another guy who has crossed and help the last guy pull over. Manish asked Punit to climb on his back and reach out to the top of the wall, Punit picked up a stick so that he can avoid those wires while climbing on top. While Punit was trying to avoid the wires using the stick we down below were shouting very quietly to look out for the wire. This shouting might have distracted either Manish or Punit I do not know but somehow, they lost the balance and suddenly we could see Punit coming very hard on the ground and we all started laughing. Suddenly we could hear Punit shouting "Abbey saalon hans rahe ho yahan mera paon toot gaya" (Guys you are laughing, and it seems I might have a broken leg).

And we realized he is in pain, added reason that we must climb inside. We somehow managed to avoid the wires and climbed to the other side. It was dark and we must carry Punit as well, as he could not walk. We tried to be very light footed to reach out to our room but because of darkness we could not see and struck a steel bucket lying there.

Suddenly a big noise and the lights of the owner room were switched on, we rushed to a spot where we can hide ourselves. No one came out it seems the owner may have glanced from the window and then again, the light went off and we went to our room.

Next day we took Punit to the doctor and he suggested to put some crape bandage and take rest (Thank God no broken leg, just the swollen feet with pain). We came back, and the owner asked what happened?

We guys could not avoid laughing at this question and the expressions on Punit's face was

MC lll

RAGGING

The word Ragging, just the mention of it will bring horrible things in front of everyone Mind and Memories. Well that is not the case here.

Every coin has two different sides (Unless the coin is compromised!), it depends on person/society/civilization which side they want to use.

Nuclear energy if used properly could remove all the energy related issues, but if applied for devastation could result in Hiroshima and Nagasaki.

One more thing, the Joy or sorrow associated with the outcome of an event or action is totally dependent on the person's emotional quotient or conditioning through which he or she has gone through his or her lifetime.

I, for example could get little disturbed because of certain event, Action or outcome whereas some other person could be in mental imbalance under the same circumstances. Ultimately a progressive society always thrives to be even to all the people who belongs to it and decides which practices are good and which should not be followed as it could lead to different trauma levels. Same is the case with Ragging and that is why I feel it was appropriate to ban it.

To be true to myself I really miss those days of Ragging during my college days. Finally, I got placed in a college down south in a city called Chikamagalur. None of the prestigious professional colleges were ready to handle my intelligence and that's why no one offered me a seat.

Those were the days when ragging was quite common in professional colleges and we were told about so many horrible stories about what happens during Ragging time.

During my counselling when I came to know about the college I have to Join, I reached out to my acquaintances to find someone who is already studying in that college (Thinking this will help me to overcome the Ragging trouble, later on when reality struck I came to realize nothing stops you from being Ragged). I came to know about a guy who was studying in that college at that time, his name was Raghu and I talked to him. He assured me of all the help and told me about how nice the college is and that I should not fear anything and will help me out. He told me that I should meet him in Room Number 206 in the boy's hostel when I reach there.

With a very relieved mind I packed my baggage and took a bus to Chikamagalur from Bangalore.

I went to Boys Hostel and Knocked on the door of Room Number 206, a lot of noise was coming from inside the room. Suddenly the door was opened, and a chubby looking guy came out with a razor in one hand and half shaved beard looking at me enquiringly all over and suddenly without listening to me he shouted 'Abey naya murga aaya hai' and he pulled me inside.

There were few guys inside the room all laughing and asked about me. I Played a bit smart there and instead of telling them that I am here for Admission, I told them that I am looking out for Raghu in 2nd Year for admission of one of my friends. Hearing this all of them apologized and told me that I am in the wrong hostel, I should be looking for Raghu in Senior's hostel. For fresher the college were having a separate hostel. That smartness at least saved me from that initial round of batchmate ragging (Later on I came to know, the guy who came out was named Dheer and they would have ragged me at that time had I not told them a different story).

So, I picked up my baggage and went to Senior's hostel and knocked at Raghu's door, he welcomed me asked for my well-being and helped me a lot to settle down in college.

I shared a room with 2 other boys in the fresher hostel.

Ragging follows different tradition and (I would say politics) in different colleges, for my college it was divided into two groups North Indian and South Indian group. North Indian fresh joiners were supposed to be ragged by only North Indian seniors whereas South Indian fresh joiners of the group were supposed to be ragged by only South Indian seniors. This not at all means that they cannot stop new joiners from other groups, but every business has a set standard and rules which are followed as religion and should not be broken.

The other rule of ragging was that the Just Seniors (2nd Year Students) have the right to rag and new joiners and others (Super Seniors) will call as and when required (Mostly when they are getting bored and to show who is the dominating group or boss). Fresher were supposed to wear full shirt buttoned up to collar, trousers (No jeans) and as soon as the last evening class finish everyone was divided into slots about from which flat, they have the ragging call.

Ragging was not allowed in hostel, but as first year goes by most of the student used to move out from hostel and take a rented flat outside hostel because of the food quality and independence they would like to have.

After 5 PM every day we were told that different group of people are called by different Just seniors in different flats.

At first, I was worried, used to spend full day in college and the come back and spent the entire evening till 9:00 PM with seniors for ragging. Not getting enough time to go through the subjects which were being taught. But now when I look back, I think those were the most fruitful days of my college in terms of study, fear of not getting enough time to study and lagging behind forced me to study as much as I can during that time (This dedication towards study never came for my entire college duration).

That day when I came back from my classes in evening, everyone was in hurry. I was told that everyone is called in Flat 126 for 'Shiv Pooja' and all of us are required to be in the flat by 6:00 PM. This was a direct call from our Just Seniors and all of us were in hurry, we completed our evening snack hastily and then I went to my room to get dressed in proper fresher attire.

I ran towards Flat 126 as all my batchmates were already gone, knocked on the door as it was closed, and I could see Raghu opening the door. He pulled me inside and closed the door, the scene inside was totally out of my imagination. I could see all my batchmates standing Naked, before I could digest the intensity of the scene raghu was shouting 'Chal be kapde utar aur line mein khada ho ja' (remove your clothes and stand in line). That was first time in my life I faced such situation where I must get naked in front of everyone, I was hesitant for those few minutes but then my mind said what the hell. First time is always a pain and I learnt as we spent time that you get so accustomed and that as soon as the senior used to tell us open your pants we were ready with our underwear down and the seniors would have to say 'Abey pura besharam ho gaya hai kya underwear kyun khola Ill'.

One of my batchmate who was taller than others, standing Naked with his legs apart and all other batchmates were required to go inside his legs kneeling and knocking his balls as if they are knocking on the Temple bells. Few of the mischievous guys in our batch were knocking hard on his balls which made him cry and all the seniors laughing and shouting.

After passing through the 'Temple Doors' everyone has to sit on a chair with the seat colored in red paint and then put their ass on the drawing sheet to get the ass impression on the sheet.

Then we all were going to each of our just seniors one by one to get the print certified and get the marks on the print, hilarious isn't it? Your ass being rated!

There was a Just senior from Ratnagiri (Madhya Pradesh) dark black in color and very lean with below average height. If he is on road, I could slap him without any fear of being bullied, but the power of position was on his side. We feared the most of him, anything wrong or order not followed would result in one of the loudest howling from him. As if all hell is breaking and he would keep on shouting to the loudest of his pitch. We used to call him 'Kala Chor' (Black Thief).

During my early college days, I made friends with 3 guys and we were very close together. I, Shakeb, Manav and Vikrant. Shakeb was living in Flats as his brother Jamil sir was there and he was part of a group who has dominance over the North Indian, he was having some backing from the local Chikamagalur people. The other part was controlled by another guy named Ratan having support of some other guys like Unity Singh and Kaushal Sir.

I was not knowing all these details that time when I become friend with Shakeb. As I was seen quite often with Shakeb, so people thought I belong to Jamil sir group Ill.

Some demographic politics.

Localities or people who were local of Chikamagalur has a very clearly defined rule that because of college student they are not going to fight with each other which allowed them to keep dominance over the college students. Whenever a fight occurs between different college groups someone from those group will flaunt their local connection to win over. It was all about who is having stronger and better connection than other. Jamil Sir was having a very good connection with local groups whereas Unity Singh and Kaushal sir also boasts of them.

In our college Ragging has three major rituals or milestones apart from daily ragging, those were Shiv Pooja along with Ass Stamping, Mass Ragging and Fresher Party. Fresher party is the way when officially the end of ragging is announced, and you are inducted into the local college tribe.

After Shiv Pooja we spent lot of nights grouping together and laughing out on the Ass Stamps, you will not believe but we were asking each other on who has got the best marks on his imprint.

Ragging is the time when you find the best of your friend (Probably), I, Shakeb, Manav, Manoj and Vikrant became very good friends during that time. Among us Shakeb was the only guy who was not residing in hostel but used to spent most of his time in hostel only because of us.

During one of those evenings we five went up to the hostel rooftop as usual, but that day was different as Vikrant brought a Smoke with him that day which was tipped with menthol. He asked us to try it out and feel the coolness of menthol while inhaling, we all looked at him surprisingly (Smoking was considered bad as always) but then what the hell, far away from home ready to break most of the barriers!

That was the first day of our smoking and then after that we use to collect (Theft!, Hafta wasooli Ill) 25 paise from each of our batchmates room (spread around in the corners as no one cares about 25 paise) and buy a Menthol cigarette from a nearby shop outside our hostel, that coolness of menthol and the feeling of really coming out of age (When smoke comes out of your nostrils and mouth was a sight to see) instigated us to do this daily. Today I continue to smoke whereas the main culprit Vikrant who started all this left smoking after few weeks saying he is not enjoying, What an Asshole Ill

As I told earlier the problem of Local and Students of the college was ugly and visible for all of us. Everyone in the college (Especially those from Up North of India) make sure that they do not indulge in any kind of altercations/fight with the local people (Including Auto Wala's specially) there, as that would lead to pretty bad consequences.

In our hostel there were many attendants who were there to work as helping hand to the hostel administration. One of those guys (I forget the name after so many years) used to man around the main entrance gate of the hostel and check out for guys who try to gain unauthorized entry inside the hostel. Shakeb was not living in hostel but used to roam around with us in hostel almost always, that guy on the main gate has few times noticed this and cautioned Shakeb about not coming to hostel and we even had an argument with him on why he cannot come inside the hostel if he is the student of the same college.

After one of our late-night outing (Watching movie and roaming around in the town) we came back to our hostel all five of us and were going inside college when this guy stopped us and told that he will not allow Shakeb to enter. That was the end of our patience, we could not take any more and started arguing with him, yelling who the hell are you to stop us. Being young and a local out there he was agitated and roughed us up physically, that broke all the barrier and we all five started beating him here and there. He fell and we all ran off.

Next day onwards he used to stare at us as if he was going to do something, we also were in fear everyday what will happen next but couple more days passed and nothing happened, but the fear remained there and then suddenly some unexpected thing happened. We noticed that the guy was not coming to hostel every day for his job we enquired what happened to the guy on the main gate? Warden informed us that he left the job and felt the relief of our life. But that relief was for very short period.

One day we panned for an outing and after our class (No ragging call was on that day) were waiting for an auto to go to town, we saw an Auto approaching and signaled to stop. Auto stopped in front of us and to our dismay what we saw was that the same guy who we beat that day in hostel was driving the Auto with the brown dress on.

He was smiling very mischievously at us, asked us how we are doing. We smiled sheepishly…but were not boarding

on his auto.
He asked us what we are waiting for get onboard (Think about guys, one of our enemy who was a Local now become Auto Wala), Even India Pakistan enmity would fail here Ill
He started talking with us and said don't worry guys I forget that incident which happened that night, that was heat of the moment. Those words coming out from his mouth were sounding like heavenly music to our ears.
We said sorry to him about that incident and with relief carried on, That was the day and till the time I remember of my college life now we remained in each other's good book and he always use to stop by us whenever he sees and spent some time chatting together.
Time flew and we were so busy with the new environment and Ragging that when the semester end started knocking our door we never knew.
Now is the time of Mass ragging, we came to know this is a mega event and everyone must participate and do activities. We were specially instructed to bring our Ass Stamps with us. Our college is surrounded by Hills and on that Sunday, everyone was told to gather in a flat from where we must track to a location on top of the hill. We packed our bag with some water bottles and dressed up in our fresher attire and started our Journey all laughing and giggling about upcoming event. Our seniors were shouting and trying to terrify us, but by this time we were so associated and close to our seniors that they also knew those will have no effect.
Our just seniors were ahead of us and roaming around on the hilltop around bushes to look out for ideal place. We were suggesting all places we can, but they were looking

for place which is kind of hidden among bushes and secluded.

Once they identified the spot, we all were asked to take rest and have our breakfast. We were chatting and giggling with each when suddenly Kala Chor shouted in his screaming sound to stand up and make a long line. We all could sense the change in stance and tone of our seniors and understand that we need to follow now.

Once we were all in line, seniors positioned themselves around different portions of that long line.

Then came the order to undress from tip to toe. Everyone was asked to grab the Penis of the boy standing at back of him with 1 hand and the balls of the boy in front with other hand making a chain Ill

I know it sounds very different! But that was the moment of our life where we enjoyed so much. Order was to start the train, and no one must break the chain and move from one station to another mimicking the sound of train. Every station was manned by a senior. As soon as the train started moving, we guys started having grand masti Ill Guys in front pulling hard whereas guys in back squeezing. Batchmates felling down, breaking chain laughing and crying hard at each other and our seniors all laughing with tears rolling down.

Suddenly we heard the noise of shouting from the nearby bushes, we all were terrified. Seniors asked us to put on our uniforms and we all rushed to see the nearby bushes if anyone was there. We could not see anyone out there.

Everyone came back and then we were asked to submit all our Ass Stamps to decide on the winner.

A Bengali guy with big bum was the winner of Ass Stamp competition. Evening approaching, we wrapped up and

that was the official end of our ragging days.
Next day we came to know that our seniors were called by Principal as someone complained to him that women who went in jungle to collect dry branches saw a lot of naked students standing (I mean more than 50 naked penises hanging around!!!). As he could not get it verified (No one testified from our batch) he served a strict warning and then let them go.

PADOS KA BHOOT (GHOST AT OUR NEIGHBOUR'S HOUSE)

When we were young (during our preteen days) there was a certain fearful fantasy about Ghost Stories. I still remember watching horror show and movies like 'Kile ka Rahasya' or say 'Evil Dead' during night with our face hidden behind our palms or pillow to protect ourselves from the sudden appearance of Ghost or Ghost Sound and yet trying to watch.

While sleeping all those horror events coming to life as if they are going to catch on me which will keep me awake and force me to switch on the lights while lying in bed with my eyes open so that no one or nothing comes sneaking from the dark.

During our childhood days there were no Idiot Box, and electricity used to play a lot of hide seek with us. Which gave us ample dark nights (Perfect Environment) to be fearful and enjoy those ghost stories cuddling with siblings and our parent and uncles who used to be the storyteller.

I vividly remember one such night when after dinner we were sitting on our veranda with our maternal uncle in a dark night with no lights. He was narrating to us the incidents which supposedly he witnessed about ghosts. That was such a fearful and yet such an exciting night that I could still remember the feeling of that fear till today.

Another one which my Masi (My mother's sister) told us was about how she witnessed the eyes of a boy watching her from down under the bed which tops everything and even today while sleeping if my hand goes down my bed and I wake up I pull it up fearing someone will catch it from down under the bed. Oh my god! Just think about it two wide open eyes in dark watching at you from down under your bed!

When you ask, most people would say they do not believe in ghost. There is no scientific evidence to suggest that there is something called ghost (probably), and yet you have so many stories floating around all over the world about them. I am also one of those who will say they do not believe though I am a witness of one such event which happened at a house just adjacent to us.

Now a days it is not so prevalent but during those days when we were children there used to be very strong bond between neighbors. We used to live as if we were blood relations, sharing and caring for each other not only in our joys and sorrows but in our day to day life.

I was lucky to have a neighbor with whom I have spent a large part of my childhood memories. A lot of my time was spent with that family which was from down south. We created such a strong bond that I started calling him 'Nana' (Mother's Father), probably that is the reason why I am so fond of Idli, Dosa and other south Indian dishes. My taste bud was fed by those people and are now fond of that taste.

Slowly we started growing up and he started growing old and his next generation started living there (His son got Job in his place and they continued living in the same house). Sundar Chacha, Nana's Son was a very arrogant and yet the most caring person I have ever come across in my life. He got married to a very young girl, a good example of what you call South Indian beauty. We brother and sister become very good friend of Chachi (we were in our teens and she probably have just passed her teens). She was not knowing Hindi (Tamil was her mother tongue) and we take pride in teaching her Hindi.

I am telling all these because the events which I am going to narrate has Chachi as the central character.

It all started with few light bulbs were not found on their place when we wake up in morning at Chacha's house. Initially we dismissed these as rare occurrences of some mischievous kids of the locality.

Suddenly the frequency of bulbs getting stolen increased and Chacha would have to buy new set of bulbs every couple of days. We started enquiring and even threatening some of those bad ass kids who in our view were the potential suspect who could be doing that.

All of them pleaded innocence and told us that they do not have any idea if this kind of things are happening at his house.

We all were clueless and surprised that how could the bulbs are gone without anyone noticing? Buying new bulb every other day was creating a lot of financial trouble as well for Chacha.

We decided to keep night vigil to find the thief who were stealing those bulbs. We went to roof top and slept there so that in night when the person come, we can catch him red handed during the act.

It seems the thief was smart enough to know about our plan and on those days when we are on night vigil bulb remain there. With every passing day we were getting frustrated as we were not able to catch the thief and yet when we were not on night vigil the bulb was off the place. Even more surprising was the fact that this was not happening at any other house some the thief has special attraction for the bulbs at Chacha's house. While these events were happening on the other side Chachi's health was getting bad, she was having stomachache, fever and was vomiting a lot.

We formulated another plan and put live wires with current around the boundary of the house so that if anyone tries to trespass would get a shock of lifetime (It was not possible to be on rooftop every other day).

Again, no result and now the bulbs are gone every day.

It was one of those Morning when we were at Chacha's house talking to each other and looking at the empty bulb holder, when I thought of roaming around the house perimeter to see if there is something, and I could see those bulbs lying there outside the courtyard under tree roots and garbage.

This was a new development for us, who will do such kind of thing? Stealing and then hiding it around the house itself?

Now every day in morning we use to search for the missing bulbs, and we could find few of them as well as some of them broken.

Chachi's health condition was getting worse day by day, for few days she will be ok but then again, she will go through the same cycle of fever and vomit. Chacha consulted a lot of doctor and tried so many medicines (Allopathy, Ayurvedic, Homeopathic…) but not result.

This kind of become regular and part of our life and we

almost started living with it (Including Chacha). I cannot resist myself sharing a funny incident which happened during those days, but when I look back and recall that incident, I am almost certain that it happened because there was help from that thing which was there.

It was a normal afternoon and my two sisters were in the back courtyard of our house passing out idle time. There was more than 100 ft. distance from our backyard to Chacha's backyard and somehow these two girls come up with a bizarre idea of throwing a stone on the bulb at the back courtyard of Chacha's house and break it to create a sensation. They were not even an average shooter and even in their wildest dream they can never think of hitting the target from such a long distance but then they were up for a mischief and they aimed and whirled a shot for the bulb.

Bingo! And that was like one of the wildest shots which comes off on an odd day, and the stone hit the target and the bulb goes down with a big sound of Vacuum breaking out with glass. They were stunned for a moment and then screaming they ran inside the house all trembling on what they have done.

Was that a mere coincidence or some invisible Hand of God…Errr…Ghost working behind the scene?

As it always happens regular cannot remain regular for long in anyone's life. There will be change and there must be change whether it's God or Ghost or Humans Ill. On a side note we noticed that whenever these incidents of bulb missing were happening Chachi's health deteriorated and she remained bed ridden during all those times. In India it's a common practice to dry our clothes in sunlight by hanging them in the back of our courtyard.

One fine day when we were having our lunch, we heard very loud voice of Chacha probably arguing with someone. We rushed out of our house to see what happened. Chacha was having very heated altercation with the neighbors who were living opposite of his backyard. I could see all those clothes which Chacha has hanged in the backyard for drying were dirty with mud and filth and there was a lot of garbage scattered all over his backyard.

Look Minku what these guys have done to our clothes and backyard, he was telling me with a lot of rage and anger. Chachi was vomiting there and telling me to call Chacha inside and not to fight.

I consoled Chacha and somehow managed to get him out of that place and then checked with those people living opposite to his house if they could have done this kind of stuff?

They swear in the name all the holy gods they follow that why would they do such kind of stuff? There was no animosity between them, and everyone was living happily. I somehow talked and pacified them, told them that Chacha is already going through a lot of mental agony.

This garbage throwing which even has human shit at times started happening every now and then. We all were very depressed not knowing what we can do. On one side these incidents of bulb missing and garbage throwing and on the other side taking care of Chachi as he was really suffering.

During one of these conversation of what we can do, once of the learned member (Aged ones) of the community suggested that these events do not seem normal and there seems to be some kind of bad omen or really bad spirit present in this house and we should seek out the assistance of spiritual healers (Ojha's) in order to get out of this trouble.

Being a part of community having scientific mindset how can I believe on those superstition? I outrightly rejected that idea and instead asked everyone to consult a good doctor for Chachi and keep a vigil for people who were doing those mischief.

With every passing day I myself started doubting the whole idea of rationale behind every event and was bending towards the idea of alternate approach.

Finally, Chacha gave up and decided to approach some healers to get rid of that invisible force which is creating all these mess. There is a community in India who are supposed to be very deft at these kinds of activities and boast of their achievements through neighborhood people for advertisement.

We reached out to one of the Maulvi and he agreed to perform the healing ceremony at Chacha's house that night. Ceremony was to start at 8:00 PM, Chacha's house was packed to the inches. Maulvi was sitting in the room and murmuring something very slowly can be observed by watching his lips movement only, nothing could be heard. He was moving around the entire house with a broom made up of peacock feather waving it in air over people as if trying to find something. Finally, he sat beneath the bed on which Chachi was lying (because of ill health) looked at her intensely and then gave a sudden cry "JINN HAI" (In India bad spirits are known by many names, JINN, CHUDAIL, BHOOT, PISACH etc. You can write a whole book just describing the attributes of all of them).

He told there is a Jinn who is fond of Chachi and is living with her and do not want anyone to come near her. He told us he will catch him put him inside the bottle (showed us an empty beer bottle) and we will have to go near the bank of a nearby river and dig deep and put that bottle inside it so that this Jinn can never come back.

He reached inside the handbag which he has brought with himself and placed few steel plates in front of him. Wrote some puzzles on all of them in Urdu and asked us to nail them on each of the doors and windows of the house.

He then put a lot of stuff which were associated with the ritual like (Lemon, colored rice, flower petals, etc.) and lit camphor in a small container in his left hand and put few stuffs in that which started producing fumes.

He then started chanting something in his mouth in Urdu which we could not understand and waving his broom so that the smoke coming out of that camphor pot goes towards Chachi. With every moment he was getting louder and louder and started moving his upper portion of the body and head very vigorously in a circle. With all his long hair flowing as he was moving with his black robe inside that camphor fume filled room, the scene was more like he himself was the bad spirit in the room.

But then after few seconds he picked up the bottle which he showed to us and started yelling to come inside the bottle in the name of Allah (God) and put a camphor inside the bottle. And then he suddenly stopped yelling and very hurriedly grabbed the bottle cock and sealed it very tight.

With a victorious look he announced to all the audience available in the room that he caught the Jinn and is inside the bottle, anyone want to see can see it.

And that was it everyone was now trying to get a glance of that Jinn in the bottle. I also got my chance to see the bottle and I could clearly see a kind of floating human like creature made up of fumes in that bottle. I could not believe that I am telling this, but I did saw that thing in the bottle. We all were so ecstatic that finally we are out of trouble and we went to the bank of river and dug very deep to bury that bottle inside it. Maulvi took his money and told us that Chachi will also start feeling better now as he has removed the bad spirit from the house. He also cautioned us not to remove those steel plates with jigsaw puzzle as they will act as barrier for any of those bad spirits to come inside the house again (What will happen if the spirit is waiting outside the houselll). Well you gotcha! For outside house you have some locket with those jigsaw puzzle written on a paper and folded inside the locket to protect.

Next day Morning and to our surprise nothing happened, we spent the entire day waiting for events but nothing!

Next to Next day…again NOTHING!

We were happy that everything is not on track, in some corner I was thinking I goanna miss those James Bond days of tracking the missing link. Just wanted to add, these things went on for years and not for a single day anyone of us apart from Chachi was troubled in anyway by that invisible thing. We never felt any kind of fear day or night living just next door or going to Chacha's house or spending our time together full of fun and activities with Chachi.

We later realized that those two days of no event was like Silence before a big thunderstorm. Because what happened after that was kind of scary at one point of time for those people who faced it.

Chachi was not feeling well and Chacha must go to office

so he asked me to be at his house for the whole day and take care of Chachi. That was the time when I was sitting idle at my home after my +2 preparing for entrance examinations of engineering.
Chacha gave me a good excuse to run off from my studies and pass off some time watching TV shows without getting scolded by my parent for not studying. I picked up those Resnick's and brilliant tutorial books and went off to Chacha's house. I remember I closed all the outside doors and switched off the light of Chachi's bedroom so that she can sleep comfortably, and I switched on the TV and started watching some of my favorite program at that time.
After around 30 minutes Chachi came rushing saying she wants to Vomit. I opened the back door for her to out and Vomit, after vomiting she came back inside, I closed the door and helped her sleep on her bed and then came back to watch TV again.
Again, after few minutes she complained of Vomiting, I opened the back door and helped her with that. She came inside and I was closing the back door when she suddenly asked 'Minku why is it so dark, you haven't switched on the lights… ' and we both at the same
moment looked at the place where the bulb was supposed to be and cried where is the bulb? She ran into kitchen and there also no bulb, I followed her towards the kitchen. Suddenly she gave a very loud cry!
Look there Minku and pointed towards the bathroom bulb and never in dream I can believe what I saw. Light bulb while on was falling slowly from its holder and getting split into two vertical halves in front of my eyes (Just like a dramatic slow-motion movie scene) and fell on the ground with a thud!

All the bulbs from inside the house are now gone, Chachi started crying. Somehow, I consoled her and put her to sleep on her bed. Even with such a scary incident happening Infront of me I never felt the fear of ghost being there. I remained there till Chacha came back from office and narrates entire incident to him. This started new set of events, where bulbs, garbage throwing has moved to next level.

Later Chacha told us that he also started losing money from his wallet and places. The severity and frequency of Chachi getting ill has intensified a lot.

It was one of those night when Chachi was very ill and my mother and sister were sitting beside her taking care of her. Chacha has gone to market to buy medicine and regular grocery stuff. My younger sister was standing on the entrance door of Chachi's bedroom while my mother and elder sister were sitting beside her on the bed giving her the care. Chacha came home with the stuff and put them inside the refrigerator which was in the same bedroom where Chachi was. After putting those stuff in refrigerator Chacha went away to change.

Suddenly my younger sister who was standing on the door of the bedroom felt or maybe for a fraction of second noticed something came out really quick like a flash from the wall and next thing she saw was the sauce bottle on floor next to the bed broken with a loud glass breaking noise and all the sauce spread on the floor.

Everyone in the room screamed and startled, Chacha came running in the bedroom with an expression I do not know if that was of surprise, Agony or Fear, or a combination of all of those.

Just now he bought that sauce bottle and put it inside the

refrigerator and to make sure that it's the same bottle he opened the refrigerator and we all can see the bottle was missing.

After this we reached out to a lot of healers to get rid of this Vexation because of that spirit but no one was able to provide any relief, finally we called Chachi's parent so that they can take her back to her home (Thinking change of place and distance would baffle the Jinn and he/she/it will go away to find new interest).

But it seems the Jinn was having different idea. Chacha bought train ticket for everyone to go back for a month. On the day of travel a cab was booked to take them to railway station from where they have to board the train, during the trip to railway station the cab got a punctured tube, they some averted a collision with a truck and were late reaching the platform because of all these incidents. Somehow the late reputation of Indian railway helped her catch the train even though they were late to the station and all of them were able to reach Chennai without any further incidents.

Even after place change, she remained ill and in bad health, after some time few violent incidents also happened there where some of the drums in the kitchen would fall off just beside the person standing.

Some utensil will come flying and stuck on the body of the people moving around.

Members of the home were really panicked and afraid and so they decided to take Chachi to a temple in some other town which was famous for getting rid of all these bad omens and ill spirits.

Chachi, her parent decided to travel during night so that they can reach the temple early morning and will have full day to go through all the rituals there. They booked the cab for travel, but Chachi was in the worst ever condition of her health she had been during all these months. Vomiting every few seconds, trembling with high fever, red eyes…. Looking at her, Father started thinking about travel but then Mother was adamant, and she forced him to take her even with that condition for the travel.

Male members of her family reached to her bedroom to pick her up and carry her to the cab as she was not in the condition to walk.

They tried to lift her from the bed but were not able to do so, she was resisting very furiously pushed one of them so hard that he feels on the floor almost like flying to a distance. Somehow all of them managed to carry her but she caught the bed with one of her hand crying I do not want to go, the grip was so tight on the bed that even after all the force and effort from those people they could drag that heavy bed few inches but were not able to carry her out to the cab.

Mother asked someone to call doctor so that she could be given and injection for sleep for them to take her to the temple.

Somehow the doctor administered the injection and they were able to move out for the other town on the cab. Few hours passed and the driver suddenly saw something on the road and tried to maneuver so that he can take the cab from the other side but he lost control (which he told us never knew how he can lose control of the vehicle, that was just a small maneuver) and they hit a tree on the side of the road very hard.

Father and the driver sitting on the front seat got hurt very badly and instead of going to the temple they must rush them to a nearby hospital for treatment.

Those incidents were more than what the family could take, and they decided to move her back and so she came back to our place once again.

This entire thing goes on for more than a year and finally we get hold of one of the healers someone told us.

He visited Chacha's house perform some pooja and asked that every member of the family living in that house (Chacha, Chachi and the kid) to sit in a circle in the bedroom with a Diya lit and placed in between and all of them should look at the tip of the light coming out of the Diya for 1 hour everyday morning and evening. I do not know how and why as I do not find any rationale behind this but after they started this ritual everything goes back to normal and from that date till now there is no trouble, and everyone is living happily.

There are lot events and things for which human are yet to find any reason or rationale or scientific explanation and almost 90% of the time you hear third party account of these incidents which make us believe that these are just stories created for sensation....But there are things which remain unexplained. This is one of those incidents which happened with me and I am the live witness.

K. V. GAYA NO. 2

We were in class 11th when Vijaya Kumar sir our geography teacher told us about an event called Youth Parliament which was supposed to happen at Kendriya Vidyalaya Gaya No. 2. No one knew what this event is all about and that was the first time our school was going to participate in this event.

Vijaya Kumar sir picked up some of the best orators and artists of our school and then he must complete the numbers to form the crew. He asked me if I am interested in this event?

I used to be an introvert and stage fearing guy always but even then, I was one of the most followed up boy in my school.

When sir asked me about the event, as expected my first instinctive reaction was no sir, I cannot do this kind of stuffs. Then he reasoned with me about how he must complete the crew and if I could participate there will be few others who will follow me. He also told me that it would be a fun event the entire trip. Living for 2 days in Gaya in a school dormitory with friends, taking bus to reach Gaya, and I realized how mischievous and fun filled trip it can be.

I nominated myself for the event and the soon I nominated there were a lot of other guys and girls who were ready to join which include Partho, Manish Singh,

Anju, Lalita, Prashant to name few of them. The situation was that Vijay Kumar sir was now in a dilemma about who should be the part of the group and who should not be.

Youth parliament is an Initiative by Government to imbibe the culture of an Ideal parliamentarian from a nascent stage. This event provides an opportunity for our Parliamentarian to understand how children perceive an Ideal parliament and parliamentarian should function and behave towards the nation. Different schools participate at the region level and the winner will then compete at the national level. Ultimately the winning team will get an audience with the government representative and will get a chance to participate in some of the live parliament proceedings.

We started practicing for the event (Regional Level), and the practice itself was such a fun as we use to get 2 hours of not attending the classes and having fun with friends together.

We divided ourselves into two group, one group representing the government and the other group representing the opposition. The government group has got all the orators and artist on that side whereas the opposition consist of we the fun seeking guys Ill.

Of course, I was the leader of the Opposition.

We rehearsed extensively and created the entire script for 30-minute session from our school.

Sir told us that we will leave by bus in evening and would reach Gaya (Birthplace of Gautam Buddha) by early morning.

Bus moved out of our school campus and we all started shouting and celebrating, Playing Antakshari*, dumb charades.

*Antakshari – This is a Hindi word made up of two parts. Ant + Akshari.
Ant, Means End and Akshari means Alphabet. It's a spoken parlor game played in India. Each contestant sings the first verse of a song that begins with the previous contestant's song selection ended.

Our bus was moving very slowly because of very busy market area when I saw a guy passing remarks on the girls sitting by the window of the bus. I shouted at the guys with some cuss words and they also reciprocated.
I and friends joined this hooliganism and from nowhere I thought and started searching for things to throw at them, couldn't find anything and suddenly I saw some foams and choirs coming out from the seat of the bus and my eyes lit with sparkle Ill.
I pulled out a lump and threw at the guys outside shouting at us and closed the window. My friends saw this, and this was fun thing to do and everyone started piling up on foam and choirs from the almost broken and filthy seats of the bus.
Everyone started throwing those lumps, guys outside were unprepared for this move and they decided to run off (Looking at numbers, shouting and the newfound way of hurting in front of girls).
All our teachers were sitting at the front (Vijay Kumar Sir, Sahi Sir, PT Sir, Supari – Our yoga teacher) and because of almost dark condition and we sitting at the rear side of the bus and our human shield in front (Made by friends) they couldn't understand what was happening with the bus. They just saw some eve teaser and we are taking them to task (Realization of what we did came when they had to

pay the bill to the bus driver Ill).

At around 9:00 PM we stopped on a roadside hotel (Line Hotel) for food and ate one of the best meals of my life. I still remember the taste of that Tandoori Roti and Tadka (Wheat bread baked in an earthen Pot and Lentils fried with Indian Spices).

Exhausted from those fun filled activities and filled stomach most of us slept for the entire trip till we reach K.V. Gaya No.2 early in the morning.

We were escorted to the School Dormitory where we were given two big rooms (one for boys and another one for girls). Blankets and beds were there to put on floor for sleeping. That was a leisure day for us as our event was scheduled for the next evening.

We went to Bodh Gaya for sightseeing. We visited the famous Mahabodhi Temple where buddha attained Enlightenment and saw the famous Bodhi Tree. The temple complex was shining like silver. So many tourists visiting the place, the complex was free of dust and noise! A rare sight at most of the temples in India.

We came back to our school dormitory in evening fully exhausted from the tour. Changed our clothes and went out for dinner in the cafeteria hall. After dinner we came back and every one of us did one round of rehearsal for the next day event before the girls move out to their own room. We laid our beds and blankets and prepared for sleeping, all the shoes and sleepers were kept on the sides and we all laid our blankets in two rows.

I along with Partho, Manish Singh and JP were sleeping together along with other members. Teacher's along with few more students were sleeping on the other row. We switched off the light and put on blanket and started chatting when JP shouted in pain "who the mother fucker has hurled the shoe in dark?" Seems one of our classmates decided to play mischief and threw a shoe and coincidently it struck on JP's head. I, Partho and Manish also started shouting "Kaun hai be MC?" and we heard sound of our friend giggling from the other row.

We picked up shoes from behind our head and threw hard towards the giggling sound and that started a mayhem. In that dark night shoes and slippers were flying in the air and we were ducking inside the blankets to avoid being hit.

Suddenly Vijay Kumar Sir shouted in pain shouting cuss word and saying who painted my ass red Ill with the boot slap?

And we three laughed and kept on throwing, shoes and slippers were flying and landing on the other side without address. Suddenly supari started yelling wait you rascals I will switch on the light and take you all to task. He switched on the light avoiding those flying missiles and suddenly everyone was inside the blanket with no movement, not sure who all were doing this, he warned everyone and switched off the light.

As soon as he switched off the light he cried in pain, "Kau hai be MC, ksine feka Joota?" (Who the Mother Fucker has threw shoe on me?).

But he cannot keep standing and he must duck and hide himself inside the blanket to avoid those flying missiles.

Soon we were out of shoes and slippers as they were lying far away from where we were sleeping (because of throwing without knowing the target). As it was a cold night no one's took the extra pain of bringing those near to continue the mischief and we decided silently for truce and everyone fell asleep with few minutes. But few other were too eager not to sleep and create some extra nuisance. One of them was Prashant or JP I do not remember, but he was awake for an hour and waited for everyone to sleep. He went inside his bag and picked up his toothpaste and very silently went over the other side of the row.

Put some paste on his hand and very deftly applied it on the front part of the Penis of Supari without waking him up.

Next day morning I wake up a bit late than other guys, but I heard sound of my friends laughing and shouting from the bathroom hall.

I ran towards the bathroom hall to understand what was happening there. Situation was hilarious; Teachers and students were inside the bathroom (Open from top) taking care of daily routine and those outside were filling up the bucket and throwing water from outside. Those inside were shouting cuss word and teachers threating of dire consequences, but of no avail. They cannot come outside without clothes. I also joined the group and it was so much of fun.

We decided to stop so that we can prepare ourselves for the rest of the day routine. JP called me, He along with Prashant was laughing their heart out looking at supari. I asked them what's the matter? Why you guys are laughing so much? Anything happened with Supari?

JP told me about what Prashant did last night. It seems applying paste on top of Penis (Slang for that is Supada Ill) would make it swell and Supari sir was shouting in the bathroom early morning looking at it and saying all those cuss words you can imagine in your dictionary. He was telling the whole story to Vijaya Kumar sir and he also laughed out hard asking him to show how it looks like. Students in our school had special affection for Supari sir, He is our Yoga teacher and used to be very hard on us. Anyone caught talking or not doing the Asanas in proper manner would be slapped hard on their back or head.

This was proper place and event to get even of all those deeds.

We all dressed up and went to the school, there we looked at the rehearsal of other school groups who were there. Girls and Boys flirted with other school members trying to find potential match.

At the dawn of dusk lights were switched on and the stage was lit for the participants to start the performance. We were third in the list, waiting anxiously for our turn. The first two groups were not that impressive, and audience were getting bored.

It was our turn and the performance we put together took everyone by surprise, we performed well.

At one point I decided to be the rule breaker and went outside the script to ask counter question as leader of opposition from the governing body, it was handled really well by the ruling party leader (Student of Class 9th of our school who is really good in Acting and Stage Performance). Judges sitting on the front also noted this sudden change which we introduced to the script and they applauded.

After our performance we came down and sat in the audience area to watch others perform. I could see most of the people in the audience congratulating us on our performance.

We were quite sure that we will be among the top two team and would qualify for the national level. Judges came on stage and announced the result and to everyone's surprise they put us on the third spot favoring their own School for the second position.

We cannot believe! No one else was able to digest the decision! But the decision was taken, and we must go with it.

Vijaya sir consoled us real hard, told us to look at the reaction of audience. How they cheered us and supported us, so let's forget this and move on.

In our team ruling party leader got the 1st prize in individual performance and I got the 3rd prize.

At least a consolation even after the setback I would say.

That night we packed our bags and boarded the bus and returned. Dull in spirit and awkward silence.

SCHOOL

Have you heard Bryan Adams singing? "…Those were the best days of my life….!".
Yes! SCHOOL, those were the best days of my life. Memories of my school (although started fading a bit now) has kept me fresh and young throughout these years of my midlife.
Teachers like P.N.Sharma Sir, Yadav Sir, Vijaya Kumar Sir, My Chemistry Sir (Forgetting his Name, but because of him my Organic Chemistry was awesome) who shaped and sculpted me to become what I am today, MANISH.
Friends like Manish Singh, Punit, Partho, JP, Manish Sinha, Manish Rai, Jyoti, Prashant, Gulabiya who were with me unconditionally during every ups and downs.
And last but not the least those MEMORIES to cherish forever. These memories enable me to sing from my soul "18 till I die".
I Started my school from a local named 'Arya Samaj'. This is a Hindi Medium school and I along with my sisters used to go to that school holding each other's hand crossing the vegetable market and a big cricket ground nearby our house.
I still remember coming back from school during monsoon time. It would rain continuously and heavily for weeks during 80's and I along with my sisters while coming back would not open up our umbrellas. All

drenched with water we used to splash over the water bodies formed on the cricket field because of the continuous and heavy rain. It would take us a lot of time to reach back home, because of the fun rain brings with it.

Then we all were moved to another school 'Little Star School' English medium, much better and sophisticated than the 'Arya Samaj'. My parents were very much focused on the education and well being of their kids and they did all that was in their capacity to provide us with the best of education and quality life.

Kendriya Vidyalaya Ramgarh Cantt. Was considered the best school of the region and every parent wanted their kids to get education from that school. School was inside the premises of Sikh Regiment Center and they provide the best of the fabric of Indian culture because of students from all the part of India going to that school for education. All those kids of Military personnel from different parts of India used to study in that school.

One of the biggest criteria which was laid out by the school for admission was that parent is having a transferrable job.

During my admission time Haque sir was the Principal of that school.

He was famous for being very educated, considerate and person with high moral values.

My parent applied for our admission in that school in class 5th. I was called for interview with Haque sir along with my parents. We went to Ramgarh at the appointed meeting time and I could not remember what happened or what was asked from me during that interview. I returned and next day the result was to be announced as who all are getting admission in the new academic year. That night my father and mother were discussing that it would be bit difficult for us to get admission as my father is not having a transferrable job although he tried to do some manipulation by showing some within the region transfer from one office to another.

Next day morning my father went to Ramgarh for the result of new academic year. For the entire afternoon I was playing outside and reciting Hanuman Chalisa (Rhyme praising Lord Hanuman) and praying that I should get admission. I climbed on top of window on the verandah of my house and reciting hanuman Chalisa when I saw my Father entering the house by opening the gate.

I could see he was smiling, and he came and put me on his lap and congratulated me for getting admission in Kendriya Vidyalaya Ramgarh Cantt.

From that day I started on a dream journey of my life which is still going on fresh in my memories.

I started my schooling at KV in Class 4th and could not remember much about that time (10-year-old kid probably). What I enjoyed most at that time was boarding on a school bus to go to school. Even better or the fun part for which we used to wait was a truck to come when the school bus breaks down. All kids would hop on the open truck, having no seat and nothing to hold on to. That was the ultimate test of maintaining balance during brake and speed and we enjoy those bumpy rides falling on top of each other during brakes and acceleration. Life is so good when we are kids, finding joy and happiness in small events and things.

Different barracks which were built to house soldiers of SRC (Sikh Regiment Center) were given to School administration to run the classes. Entire school was distributed in 4 zones. Administrative area, Primary Zone, Secondary Zone and Senior Secondary Zone.

Not much I remember about my primary school days in KV but I do remember my Hindi teacher who was also our class teacher in Class 4th. Very fair and bald person having a very hard hand as I remember his slap on my cheek (very hard). Do not remember why he slapped me that hard, but I guess I must be sleeping while sitting on the front when he was teaching Ill.

During those days' schools having fully functional toilets was kind of unimaginable at the place where we live. Because of that non- functional toilet I got into a situation at that time which carried very little impact at that time because of the age, but when I consider that situation now and see how my son behaves at this age I could imagine what an embarrassment it would have been for that little kid Manish at the tender age of 10 or 11 years.

Every day our school gets over by 1:30 PM and we all use to gather our bags and other stuffs and run towards the school bus stand where buses from different coalfield area use to collect kids. On that day, around 1:00 PM when the school was about to close, I felt the pressure in my stomach. I tried to settle it down by sitting on the bench and pressing my butts harder on the bench, but it seems nature was hell bent to come out and nothing could stop it. When I felt nothing could stop, I rushed to the toilet at the back of my class and relieved myself. I opened the tap to clean myself but to my surprise there was no water just drips coming out of the tap, I tried to use those drips to clean myself but instead of cleaning it was spreading. My kiddish mind thought that I should wipe it out and used my pants to clean myself and then tried to use the dripping water to wash off my pants. That was a really bad day for me it seems, that dripping water was gone and nothing coming out of the tap. I was holding soiled and smelly pant in my hand and crying. No one with me, I was so helpless and could not think of what I should do. Time was running out and I must catch the bus to go home. I rubbed my hand on the soil and wore that soiled and smelly pant and went to bus stand to catch the bus.

When the bus came, I ran and went inside the bus and looked out for the last corner seat for myself. Mostly the last seat is not the preferred seat and its less crowded part of the bus.

Bus started and I sat looking outside the window fearful and embarrassed. After some time, the smell started to put its effect and I could see the kid sitting beside me on the seat pinching nose and looking at me. Elder ones who were standing nearby my seat also started looking at me as by that time most of them have figured out the origination of that foul smell.

Kid sitting beside me could resist no more and moved away from the seat saying that I have soiled my pant, all those standing and sitting around me emptied the place and moved away laughing at me. I was so embarrassed that I never looked at anyone and kept looking outside the window crouching against the seat to make myself invisible.

Anyhow I reached my stand, as soon as the bus stopped, I quickly come out and ran towards my house crying out loud. I knew my mother is there at home who will understand my pain and agony and I can relieve myself of that embarrassment by crying in her lap. Ma came rushing when she heard me crying and entering in the house, she took me in her lap and started asking 'what happened'. I kept on crying, I knew I do not have to answer, and she will understand everything. She took me to the bathroom washed me clean and changed my clothes. Those gestures were good enough to make me comfortable and forget the entire incident for that day. A kid carries short term memory of bad situations and in couple of days probably I forgot that entire incident and started my routine as normal as it was before that incident.

I do not remember, but I am sure kids of the bus must have carried on that incident for a little longer and might have laughed few more times at me, but I moved on from that incident.

I was new at school and trying to get accepted into the group of kids to start getting the attention and importance, basic human nature of seeking attention and importance started unfolding into my simple and uncomplex mind. As you grow up your mind also starts to make you ready for the world by introducing new ideas and complexities which it observes on daily basis around your social networks.

Cricket was, is and will be a religion for Indians although it's not a national game for India but the importance of Cricket in India can be seen, as you move around the length and breadth of her geography.

We moved to standard 5th and I was searching for a group where I am acceptable and given due importance. Kids were fond of playing cricket during games period and at that time they bring their own ball and bat to play than to depend on school (as playing equipment's were not enough to be given to each and every class). I noticed that kids who bring the bat or ball were given a lot of importance and other kids try to cozy up with those who bring it. I know for sure that I cannot afford a professional bat purchased from the sports store as it will be too costly but then I must devise a way. Improvements, Discoveries or Innovation in most of the cases always comes out from the two extremes: People who are extremely laborious always looking out for new ways of doing things and those who are too lazy and always try to find ways to reduce their effort, both of them do have one thing in common that is to find new ways.

During earlier days (although still prevalent with washing community specially in the urban areas) for washing clothes woman used a wooden block shaped like a small cricket bat to wash of the dirt from heavier clothes like quilts and bedsheets to ease out the hard work of washing them.

The wooden block my mother was having was made of solid Sheesham wood and when I tried it with a ball, I could see the amazing stroke that 'bat' was having. I got twinkle in my eyes and I persuaded my mother to allow me to take it to school to play cricket.

Next day I was very excited, and I dressed up and picked up my new bat and rushed to the bus stand to catch my school bus. I was overjoyed thinking how I am going to dominate my group with this awesome bat.

At bus stand older students (didi and bhaiya) started smiling when they saw me holding that peculiar 'bat'. One of them even asked why you are carrying this cloth washer with you? Is there some school project you are working upon?

I giggled thinking how foolish they are and explained them that this is my bat which I will be using during our games period to play cricket and suddenly all of them started laughing. I could not understand why they were laughing…. whatever I thought, let them laugh I am going to have my king day today.

In school it was an amazing day really, all the members of our cricket group were fond of this new bat. The way we were hitting the ball towards the boundary was awesome, we really enjoyed playing and I started getting the attention I was seeking.

Children as they grow acquire knowledge and knowledge come with it's own complexities. For we kid it was just an amazing bat which hits the ball out of boundary whereas for those older students since they now know what it is, it was kind of foolishness to carry it around. They were right with the age and thinking they now have but we were overjoyed and excited from whatever we had.

That bat incident was the start of my becoming an important member of the group who all would hear, and I carried on that important position till the entire school days.

I started developing my bonding and friendship with other kids in the school and we were moving to higher classes. I and Partho were close to each other and were always leading our group in all the mischievous and fun activities.

As we grew teenage syndrome started catching up with us and we started looking at girls and painted them as 'teri wali' (yours) and 'meri wali' (mine). In our days we were mostly the members of fattu FOSLA group, our friend Punit was the only exception.

Because of recent postings two new girls joined our school from Army, Sapna and Nindiya and Partho was all out for Sapna (As I told you we were FOSLA), when we say all out it means only within our group we pull partho's leg taking her name and all nothing else…at most we use to follow the girl and watch them from the nearby field while they were inside the class or moving around just trying to see if they are also looking at us or not. If for any reason they see at us for few seconds that would mean heaven for us.

We were also part of Scout and Guide group and at that time our school organized a two-day Scout and Guide camp. We were all excited, this was the first time that we will stay out of home with our friends in the camps at school. Fun part was that girls will also be there and an apt time for those mischievous things to carry on.

I and Partho were in the same camp along with other members of our group. We were really enjoying and teasing each other, just next to our camp starts the girls camp and Sapna was also there in that camp.

Perfect place and opportunity for us to tease Partho and daring him to go and talk. Nothing happened all day and Partho was upset with our regular teasing. Lastly, he told us to wait for night to see how daring he is. He planned that late at night when everyone is sleeping in their camp he will enter the girl's camp and will kiss Sapna. We really made fun of him when we heard this, that was impossible even in our wildest dream.

But Partho was really on it and determined, he asked me to come along with him. I was a real big fattu specially when it comes to girl and the kind of act which Partho was planning I cannot in my wildest imagination could think of doing that. I do not know but my fear of getting caught and the aftereffects would never allow me to do that.

Partho told me not be afraid everyone will be sleeping at

around 2:00 AM in the night, they will not even know. I kept on saying no. Then he told me ok wait and see I will just go inside roam around and come back nothing will happen then you will come with me. I agreed thinking that Partho will not do that. To my surprise Partho went inside the girl's camp remain there for few seconds and come back. Those few seconds were like hours for me, fearing anytime I will hear screaming and voices of girls and Partho will be running around. But nothing happened and he came outside. Then he caught me and started dragging me with him to show how he is going to kiss Sapna inside. I was so afraid, I begged him to leave me and he was dragging but then he finally gave up and instead asked someone else to go along with him.

I do not know what they did when they went inside but Partho came back and told me that he messed up. He removed his blanket which he was putting on himself to disguise while he was kissing Sapna and she opened her eyes. Both ran off like hell back to the camp.

We all never slept that night thinking what would happen now. Next day we were fearing anytime principal would come to us, we were not even looking towards the girl's camp to avoid Sapna looking at us. But nothing happened and we went back to our home.

Next day as soon as I reached to class from the bus stand, Partho was standing there in front of me all trembling and fearful. I asked what happened and he told me that Sapna's father came in military jeep (having big moustache a colonel in Army) and is inside Principal room.

Partho was almost crying that anytime principal is going to call us and would terminate us from the school, what her father is going to do we cannot imagine. We were waiting for that time but somehow the clock kept ticking but that moment never came. His father came out and rode off his jeep out of school and we never even got a call from the principal. Probably Sapna never told anyone about this or whatever but from that day we put fingers on our ears and swear that not again.

During winters it would be cold inside the class so our teacher would take the entire class outside in the ground under sun and teaches us there. Those were the days we really look forward to and that happens to be the best period of our school. Going out in the playground during study period and sitting on the ground in groups and circles under the sun was real fun. The more exciting reason for us to be in ground was 'Mastram'.

Mastram is a codename very famous in India for hindi porn stories. For any cheap hindi porn book if you look at writer's name it will be Mastram. During our 8th/9th class that was the first time someone introduced to the group about this exciting book. Everyday in class there must be someone with some new variation of book which we would read secretly during our free time or even during class time if sitting on back bench.

I specially remember a particular day. Our regular Hindi teacher was on leave so par time responsibility to manage the class for that period was given to our Yoga teacher who was famous with our group because of his peculiar way of talking. We nicked him 'Supari'.

We were told that people who chew a lot of Supari (In India supari chewing is a habit) get a thick tongue and are not able to spell properly. They used to spit a lot while talking and that was the case with Supari sir. He asked the class to move to the playground under sun and he will take

the class there only. That was the fun moment we were waiting for.
Everyone rushed to the ground screaming, shouting, fighting, and giggling with fun. Our group decided to take a far corner of the ground and sat in circle. Supari was running here and there shouting all should gather at one place, but we begged and insisted that we should sit like this. He agreed to our demand instead of arguing and wasting his energy on a part time class.
We sat in circle and I took the center of the circle. Supari told us to get our hindi book and read a particular chapter. Everyone in our group opened the Hindi book and I was handed over the Mastram. I put that small porn book inside my hindi book and started reading out the story to the group. With every porn word we were laughing out like anything. That 1 hour we were laughing so much hearing that story and looking at each other that we got stomachache.
We did our first mass bunk when we were in class 10th. A very hit movie named 'Shiva' came during that time which was a big hit among teenage students because of the stunt scene where the hero pulled out the chain of the cycle to smash the villains. We went to school but after departing from bus we ran off to the theater which was our meeting point. That was the start of our bunking routine and then we bunked again (Not the entire class but a small close group) for the first time to see a morning show (Soft porn). After watching the movie we were coming back all laughing in our school dress when Manish Singh's elder brother saw us. Next day when we came to school Manish told us how embarrassing it was for him during dinner last night. Everyone in his family was sitting and having dinner

when his brother told about we bunking and watching porn movie and everyone in his family started scolding him.

With all those fun and mischief everyday almost, we moved to class 11th. I, Manish Singh, Manish Sinha, Partho, Punit, Prashant, Pikesh, Manish Rai and Jyoti formed a closely knit group of friends who were always the center of attraction for the entire school.

During our class 11th famous Alkushi Kaand happened. It was quite embarrassing for the mastermind Prashant Pandey that time.

'Alkushi' is a wild plant very prevalent in the wilds of Jharkhand. It has tamarind like shape but if it touches anyone's skin it will create extreme itching and pain which can go on for hours if you do not apply some antidote like cow dung or take some medicine like Avil etc.

Don't know why and how but a very ridiculous idea formed inside Prashant's mind which he never discussed with us as he knew that we will not approve of it. He asked some of the naughtiest guys in the class to come along with him to execute that idea.

Every morning during prayer time all the school will assemble at the ground for prayer and assembly and there will be routine monitor assigned for every class who will guard the class during the assembly time. That day it was prashant's role to guard the class when he along with some of those guys went to the nearby jungle and brought those Alkushi fruits along with them. They rubbed it on all the girl's benches as well as on some of the front benches of those guys who he hated.

After the assembly was over everyone came back to the class to start preparing for the first period. Everyone was doing their routine core laughing and talking when suddenly the girls started murmuring, few of them stood up from the seat itching and looking at the bench. After few minutes we saw all the girls rushing to the back of the class which was walled and secluded.

They started itching and screaming itching their skin red, some of them even rubbed cow as one of the plan masterminds told them it was Alkushi which is causing this effect.

All of us were surprised and ashamed as who did this, asking each other. Principal and our PT Teacher came rushing to the class and asked all of us to leave the class. They enquired about the incident and ultimately were able to find the culprit behind the incident. We also by now knew that it was Prashant.

Next day was really embarrassing for Prashant. After the assembly, Principal sir specially announced Prashant's name and told him to come in front of the entire school assembly. He told everyone about the shameful act which he did last day and how embarrassing it was for the girls.

PT sir removed his belt and started beating Prashant in front of the assembly. He was running and PT sir was beating him with belt like anything. After few minutes Principal sir intervened and stopped the beating, but then PT sir asked him to remove his shoes and put it over his head and run the entire assembly ground holding it on his head.

Even of today when some of we friend meet we still remember that incident laughing.

When we were in 11th, that was the age when guys get lured at girls and it was more about territory. No one was allowed to pass remark or look at girls inside our territory as it was a matter of male ego and pride for us.

People from outside school who were friend with some of our class student were interested in girls in our class. Our school campus was all open and anyone living inside SRC can come inside the school and even to the class if he/she has friends in the class. In our class there was a boy named Adesh who was having once such friend Sameer who was interested in some girl of our class. Every day during our recess time he would come to the class with Adesh and sit with him staring at girls.

Our group never knew about it as recess time was fun time for our group as we use to play games or tease girls of other classes (meri wali/teri wali kind). One of our classmates told us that these days some outsider is coming to our class daily and looking at girls. That was alarming for us and breach of territory. That day we stayed in recess and saw that the boy was sitting with Adesh and laughing looking at girls. Everyone asked me to go and ask Sameer about it and tell him not to come to school again. I felt a fear inside me (being a fattu) but then looking at the support behind me I went and asked Sameer, why are you inside class do not dare come to the school again or else….

Suddenly Sameer stood up and asked what if I will come again and slapped me hard on my cheek. I was not prepared for that hard slap suddenly and I fell in front of everyone because of that slap. My friends standing behind saw this and came rushing and started beating hell out of Sameer. Some of my friends even broke the bench of the class to pick up the wooden slab and started beating Sameer with the block. For 10 minutes we were beating Sameer with fist and blocks and he was all stained with blood. Then we picked him by his collar and threatened him with dire consequences if we ever saw him again inside the school premises.

Next day I came to school and we were doing our normal chit chat with Partho before the assembly to start. That was the time when Manish Singh came riding on his bicycle. He told us that Sameer and his friends are waiting outside the SRC gate to catch hold of Manish Sinha to avenge his beating. Someone told Manish Singh about it and he rushed to inform us.

Sameer was told that it was manish who was the leader and he mistook Manish Sinha instead of me as the person who he should avenge.

I, Manish Singh and Partho started running towards the gate of SRC to alert Manish Sinha and save him from the beating. As we reached near the gate, we saw Manish Sinha coming holding his bicycle. We felt a sigh of relief thinking that nothing happened but…

As he reached near us, he started shouting and fell on the ground. He was crying and shouting in pain telling how Sameer and his friends beaten him up outside the gate. By god's grace Manish was not having any cut or bruise and we consoled him and told him to go to class. We asked where those guys went, and Manish indicated to us that they ran off.

We then rushed outside, the gate man at the SRC gate told us that he was beaten very severely by some guys with iron knuckle in their hand. We asked where they went, and the gate man indicated where they ran off.

We started running towards that side without thinking that we are just 3 and we could be outnumbered by the group with Sameer. We saw glimpse of some guys running off and we shouted catch them, they saw us and started running inside the congested lanes to dodge us. In the meantime, Manish went to class and the news spread that Manish Singh, Manish and Partho are running behind the guys who thrashed Manish. News spread like fire in the school.

Assembly was going on and everyone was in the middle of the daily prayer, but as soon as they heard this news students started moving out from the line from the back one by one and within few minutes entire 11th class (Section A, B, C), 12th Class (Section A, B, C) and 10th Class students were running towards the main market leaving school prayer to catch hold of Sameer. The entire Ramgarh market was full of students in school dress holding sticks and rods and searching for Sameer and his group. We could not find those guys anywhere then someone told us that Sameer has fled off from the market and is hiding at his home (Inside the cantt.).

All the students asked what we should do now. I told them to move to his house and catch him there. All the students almost 100 in number ran to his house and encircled the entire house from all directions and we started shouting 'Sameer come out of house'.

We were shouting either come out or we will break and enter inside, his parent came outside pleading that he is not in house but we were not buzzing as we have confirmed it from our sources that he was hiding inside. We were deciding on to break and enter the house when suddenly we saw a military truck coming and stopping at the premises.

Our principal came out of the truck as he was told (when everyone skipped prayers and fled off) that all the students are outside searching for Sameer to beat him and avenge. Principal sir started talking to all the students and pleaded not to do so or else we will attract bad image and publicity for the school.

His parents also asked that we should forgive and forget, and they will talk to Sameer about this.

Ultimately, we decided to leave it and persuaded the students to move out. They were hesitant and do not want to leave the matter until we avenge his deeds but then we moved out.

There are so many hilarious moments and fun filled days of my school that even after a decade we left the school it was like we were living the school days. Whenever we go to Ramgarh it was our habit that we visit the school at least once. Meet our schoolteachers, sit inside the premises looking at the students and living our old days together.

Remembering our Holi and Diwali, how we use to burn 1000 sound cracker on the roads of school during assembly time, Principal sir running to find who burnt the crackers and catching those culprits.

Finally the day to leave the school came and we were handing over our autograph book to each other to take back some of the remembrance of the people who we may not even meet later or who will leave us forever.

You will always be there in our Memories Manish Singh, no matter what we are and where we are.

Finally, on the closing note one of the passions which was a fad during our autograph book days: to show your writing skills specially poetry.

This one I wrote for that unknown:

कल्पित अभिलाषा

शस्य श्यामला सम श्रृँगार, नयन नशीले नटखट अपार |
वाणी वीणा सम झँकार।
होठों पे अमृत है थिरका, गालों को लाली ने दी झिड़की।
लट घटघनघोर घटा घटरानी, मुख मासूम मृदुल मुस्कानी।
प्रियतमा की मेरी ये कल्पित छवि, कर दे निष्पलक शशि और रवि।
देख उसे होगा सौदर्य विस्मित, रति की गरिमा हो जाय रज रंजित |
रच सके नही, जिसे ब्रम्हा फिर फिर
पा जिसे हुई धरती की त्रिप्ती।
जिसे ताकता शशि शरमाता, जिसे घूरता रवि रह जाता |
लाख कोशिशों मे जान न पाया, कौन है वो पहचान न पाया।
कभि इसे देख मन मेरा भरमाता, कभि उसे देख मै हूँ घबराता |
पर तभी कोई आवाज़ लगाता,
रुक मत राही बढता चल, थक मत राही चलता चल
मिल जाएगी तुझको वह महफिल, जहां पली हो तेरी संगदिल |
तुझे देख वह कल्पित काया, कुछ शर्माई सी कुछ घबराई सी
नयनों को नयनों में डाल तुझको वह आजमाएगी |
फिर ओढ़ हया की चादर वो, खुद में सिमटेगी सकुचाएगी |
फिर तुम दोनो खो जाना तोड़ रीति-रिवाज़ों को, एक दूसरे के हो जाना जोड़ प्रीत के तारों को।

www.ingramcontent.com/pod-product-compliance
Lightning Source LLC
LaVergne TN
LVHW050420160726
843469LV00041B/1159

* 9 7 8 9 3 5 4 5 8 5 9 6 8 *